CARRIED BY SIX

By: Andrew Robinson

First published by Dog Ear Publishing
4010 W. 86th Street, Ste H
Indianapolis, IN 46268
www.dogearpublishing.net

ISBN: 978-160844-934-7

This book is printed on acid-free paper.

This book is a work of fiction. Places, events, and situations in this book are purely fictional and any resemblance to actual persons, living or dead, is coincidental.

Printed in the United States of America

Boston, Thursday 2/01/09 11:15a

Its a cold and windy day. On the street crowds of people are everywhere. Police cruisers are seen rarely if not at all. Vacant lots and abandoned buildings make up the interior of the cities most crime ridden sections. Despite all the murder that plagues the city day by day it still has one of the highest black populations in the country numbering at three million and counting. Crime around the country in all of the state capitals is so bad that there are barriers built around the cities to block off the spreading anarchy. Government buildings and hospitals are the only places guarded by the military. In the cities people live regular lives. They work, pay bills, send there children to school, save money and buy property. As far as the government is concerned, they don't give a fuck what happens to anyone as long as the money keeps flowing, legally or illegally. The city is in constant chaos. It seems only Lucifer himself would be powerful enough to bring order to this living hell.

CHAPTER 1

Dorchester, Summertime 1992 6:00P

The last kick to the head knocked him unconscious. When he woke up there was no one around. Blood covered his nose, mouth and the upper half of his white t-shirt. Slowly he climbed to his feet and began to brush the dirt from his clothes. He closed his eyes as he wiped the blood from his face with his t-shirt. Jahki was only eight years old. This was the first time he had ever been jumped. He told himself that it would be the last. As he walked home he thought about nothing but revenge. Jerome, Kavon and Big Trell. The thought of the three names made him furious.

Jahki was mad that Jerome was smaller then him and that Kavon and Big Trell were bigger and older then him. He was mad that he wasn't bigger. He was mad that he wasn't stronger. He was mad that he didn't carry a weapon. But most of all, he was mad because they treated him like he was a sucker. They seen him walking from the corner store and jumped him for no reason at all. They didn't want his money or his food. They just wanted to get a reputation.

For the first time in his young life he felt hatred, raw hatred, and it felt good. He was about three blocks from his house when a black Cadillac pulled up on him with the music blasting. He knew exactly who it was in that 81 Deville on chrome Dayton's. It was an older guy from the neighborhood they called Hurt. He rolled the tinted window down and grinned so wide the sides of his mouth looked like they touched the corners of his eyes. But when he seen the blood all over the little boys shirt his grin disappeared. He put the car in park, flung the door open and stepped out. Hurt was six foot eight, bald headed, brown skinned, had big shoulders, a huge chest and arms that looked like they belonged on a guerilla.

His face looked like it was made of stone because it never had any expression on it, it was just cold and distant. The streets nicknamed him Hurt because he specialized in hurting cats his size and bigger with little to no effort. He walked over to Jahki and spoke calmly, "Who did this?" "Big Trell, Kavon and Jerome," said Jahki, with his hands in his pockets. Hurt opened the passenger door and motioned for him to get in.

After closing the door Hurt walked to the driver side and hopped in. "I just seen them five minutes ago on Blue Hill. Its time to set shit strait," he said. Making a sharp u-turn the Caddy sped away flying up West Cottage St. "Go in the glove box," said Hurt. Jahki opened the box and spotted a rusty old ice pick with duct tape on the handle. He picked it up and looked at Hurt. Hurt looked back at him and said, "This time you make them bleed." Jahki didn't give a fuck which one he caught. He just wanted to catch one of them.

The Cadillac stopped at the corner of West Cottage and Blue Hill just in time to see the three boys going up Shepard St.

Hurt made a right on Shepard and pulled over halfway down the street. Big Trell's house was at the end of the street and they would all have to pass by the Caddy to get to it. As soon as the car stopped Jahki flew out onto the side of a run down one family building. After a couple minutes went by his three targets came up the street speaking loudly about who they wanted to fuck and what girls were on their dicks at school.

Jahki waited like a venomous snake timing its attack. *Seven, six, five, four, three* he counted to himself as they passed by. *Two, one.* At the count of one he shot from the side of the house and went straight for the one in the middle, it happened to be Big Trell. He was the biggest one of the three and was also the leader. Jahki remembered what the older guys from the neighborhood use to tell him about war. They always said, "*kill the head and the body will fall.*"

With the first stab he hit Big Trell in his right kidney. The young boy let out a cry but it was muffled by the stab he took to his windpipe. Before Kavon or Jerome knew what happened Jahki hit Kavon in the right temple and was on his way to Jerome. He tried to run but Jahki was on him like flies on shit. With one quick stab downward Jahki caught him in between his shoulder blades. Jerome fell to the ground trying to reach his hands behind his back to grab his wound. Jahki kicked him in his mouth so hard his teeth came through his bottom lip and blood poured all over his chin.

The third blow was a stomp to the forehead followed by about a dozen more just as powerful as the first. Jerome was unconscious after the fourth stomp and dead to the world by the tenth. He was only seven years old but died like a grown man for the decisions he made. Like clock work, out of nowhere came Hurt speeding so fast Jahki thought he might get hit by the big car. He jumped in huffing and puffing as the Cadillac sped off. Jahki looked out the back window and watched the bodies fade in the distance. Hurt lit up a cigar, stared at the rear view mirror, turned the music on low and said, “Lil nigga, you a natural born killa.”

CHAPTER 2

Roxbury, Friday 3/21/09 10:00p

"Yo Butch!" shouted Hazel from the kitchen as she put the finishing touches on the honey backwood she just finished rolling. "Hurry up, shit by the time we get to Washington Park ain't nobody gonna be out there." "Hold your horses," mumbled the brown skinned stocky young man while putting on his grey hoody. "As fast as you drive getting somewhere late is impossible." He was Hazel's older cousin and he loved her to death. To him, she was his little sister and to her he was big bro.

Butch and his mother, Niah, were all she had after her parents died in a car crash. Only two years old when she lost her parents, she didn't even remember them to miss them. Butch's father split when his mother was five months pregnant. As far as he was concerned the man didn't exist. Now teenagers, Butch and Hazel were inseparable because of the past they shared.

They acted so much alike that at times his mother swore they were the same person.

Grabbing his twin glock nines and stuffing them into his hoody pocket, he was ready to go. "Come on," called Butch, making his way out of his room and into the living room. "You been rolling that blunt for hours now. There's probably holes all in that shit," he joked. "Yeah right," said Hazel, with a half smile as she left the kitchen and headed down the hallway for the front door. "This blunt is rolled so tight its gon choke the shit out the first nigga to hit it. You could bet on that brah," she continued, holding the blunt in front of her face like the doctors held the needles on tv.

"Take yo ass down stairs," laughed Butch, while brushing his hair and fumbling for his keys. He checked the apartment before he left, making sure all the lights were off and windows were locked. Everything was cool. He locked the door behind himself and walked down the stairs like he had all the time in the world. Older cats from the block hated the way he carried himself. They thought he was just trying to act hard. It took for a few half ass gangsters to get gunned down in the street before everyone realized that he wasn't to be fucked wit.

Dorchester, Friday 3/21/09 10:15p

"Give me the money and shut the fuck up!" barked the stick up kid while removing a large revolver from his waist. "Its two hundred dollars, its all I got, its all I got," said the young man on the opposite side of the gun. "Here, its all I got," he said for the third time quickly extending his left hand with the money in it. "Shut the fuck up! Shut the fuck up!" yelled the stick up kid, this time pointing the gun right at the mans face. "Don't shoot, don't shoot!" yelled the young man frantically.

"Didn't I tell you to shut the fuck!" Before he could finish his words the left side of his head exploded throwing blood all over the front door of the corner store.

Like routine everyone on the strip went for their guns and scrambled for cover . "Are you ok?" came a voice out of nowhere. "Are you ok?" "Yeah!" shouted the young man laying beside the dead body. "Yeah, I'm good. I'm good." "Get your money and get out of here," said the voice in a calm tone. The young man did what he was told and took off around the corner, sneakers and pants drenched in fresh blood. He didn't even half to turn around to know who saved his life. He knew by the kill, it was Detective Scott.

2 minutes earlier

What a mess, he thought to himself while turning off Geneva and making a right on Bowdoin St. The city looked like a third world country. He grew up in East Boston and never in his life did he think there'd be a day when the nations capitals looked like this. He'd been on the force thirty years now, been a homicide detective for twenty five and seen everything there is the streets got to show.

He was around to see it all from the war with China and Arabia fought and lost on American soil in 79, to the building of the barriers around the cities where the wars took place from 80 to 88, to when all the jails were shut down and the laws rewritten in 91. The law now was terminate on sight anyone caught or accused of committing murder, robbery, rape or running drug cartels. It was simple and effective. Kill, pick up the body, dispose of it. It was a risky job and the police were outgunned ninety eight percent of the time.

The other two percent they either killed the people committing the crime or lost them in a gun fight. Detective Scott and most fo the force didn't give a fuck though, they loved their job. Killing was one of the only things on earth that made sense to them. The other was making money. Scott rubbed shoulders with some of the heaviest hitters in the city and was known for his never miss one shot kill. Five foot nine, white, heavyset, grey hair, thick grey beard and that dark blue bullet proof Crown Victoria. You could spot him coming from a mile away and if you couldn't you had no business being on the streets.

The Crown Vic was just passing Jamal's Sub Shop when Detective Scott noticed a robbery on the corner of Bowdoin and Quincy St. Slowly pulling the car into an open parking spot half way down the street from the robbery, the detective slid out the car and quickly walked to the scene. Once directly across from the robbery he went for his piece, a black forty caliber fully loaded with hollow tips. The stick up kid was waiving his gun and yelling like a madman.

He was so blinded with rage that he didn't notice the heavyset white man standing in the middle of the street. Steadily aiming his piece, Detective Scott fired a single round and made his way to the dead man. It seemed to take forever but in all reality it was only seconds. He asked the man who was being robbed if he was ok. The man replied yes and Detective Scott told him to pick up his money and go.

When the man got up off the sidewalk Detective Scott noticed he was just a boy, a teenager, sixteen at the most. "What a damn shame," he said to himself, "these kids are being raised on a mine field, a corpse covered fucking mine field." While checking his surroundings he walked over to the body and picked up the big revolver that lay at the feet of the dead man. "You won't be needing this where your going buddy," said Detective Scott as he shoved the gun in his coat pocket.

Letting out a sigh of relief he grabbed his cell phone and called the station. "I got a pick up on Bowdoin and Quincy." The officer on the other end asked curiously, "One shot kill?" Detective Scott just smiled and sang into his cell phone, "*see you at the crossroads so you won't be lonely, see you at the crossroads so you won't be lonely.*" Both men laughed for a while before hanging up. Back at the station the officer stopped laughing and yelled out, "We got a pick up on Bowdoin and Quincy! Lets not all get up off our asses at once people! Come on, lets go, lets go!"

Turning to a female officer seated beside him he asked, "That Scott is one sick mutha fucka huh?" The officer, attention still in a rap magazine she was reading, lifted her eyes to the man and said, "hey, I guess you gotta be crazy as shit to last as long as he has in all this madness." The man leaned back in his chair and agreed, "I can't argue with that. You're absolutely right."

CHAPTER 3

Roxbury, Friday 3/21/09 10:20p

Washington Park was crowded as hell. Cars were double parked on both sides of the street and people were everywhere you looked. Intense ball games were being played on the courts and bets were placed by all the gamblers. The fellas came out fresh, showcasing their jewelry, new cuts and flashy cars. The ladies came out sexy as ever, as usual. Hair and nails done, skirts, belly shirts and tight jeans, some cut to perfection so just enough skin would be seen to drive the fellas crazy. The ladies definitely added all the spice to the scenery.

Clouds of weed smoke filled the air while music blasted from cars, apartment buildings and giant speakers set up on the sidelines of the ball courts. This was the place to be Friday and Saturday nights. Everybody who was somebody showed up. Sometimes the nights ended with gun fights but most of the time the brothers kept it neutral. That's just the way things were. Butch and Hazel arrived right on time taking the last double parking spot at the second ball court.

"Lets go watch the game," said Hazel, pulling out the fat blunt she saved from the house. "Lets go," said Butch, opening the passenger door to the burgundy Benz. Hazel put the blunt behind her left ear and stepped out the car like a Hollywood superstar stepping out of a stretch limousine onto a red carpet. She *was* a superstar. Tight designer clothes, perky breast, thick thighs, phat ass, five foot six, model walk, pretty face, dark brown skin, long hair tightly cornrowed and her signature hazel eyes. She was the truth.

Once they got to the ball court she sparked the blunt and coughed real hard. "I told you the first nigga to hit this is gon choke," she laughed, while still coughing. Butch wasn't laughing though, he was on alert and ready to shoot it out at any given moment. He was a real life ,modern day cowboy. Hazel didn't mind that he didn't laugh at her joke. She already knew what type of shit he stayed on. He didn't play no games.

"I'm glad you on my side," said Hazel, handing Butch the blunt. "Cause you one cold blooded nigga man, for real. If I had beef wit you I'd have to blow your house up to make sure you couldn't get back," she said, still trying to get a laugh out of him. He gave her a quick smirk and hit the blunt. "Oh shit," he laughed as he choked on the weed. "You wasn't lying cuz, you rolled this bitch to perfection." "Thank you, thank you," said Hazel. "I try to do what I can do when I can do it, you know what I mean?" "I dig it, I dig it," said Butch, while taking another pull of the blunt.

The ballers on the court were dunking and banging threes back to back keeping everybody's focus glued to the game. Butch, while passing the blunt back to Hazel was nodding his head to the music coming from the speakers when he seen his partners from the South End. Eagle, Champ and Lil Shae. Champ was a slim, grimy, dark skinned Liberian brother. Shae was Jamaican, light brown, sexy and petite and Eagle, the more devious of the three, was a chubby, brown skinned Cape Verdian cat wit a scar under his right eye.

They were all about Hazel's age, eighteen. Butch was only a few years older then them all but they looked up to him because he was the sharpest one out the bunch. He'd known the three for seven years now. They met when Eagle moved around the corner from Butch's spot back in 02. His family had just moved to Roxbury from the South End. Lil Shae and Champ came to see him everyday. Eagle met Butch at Washington Park when they were playing ball. They ran ball that whole day and been tight ever since.

One day Butch went to go check Eagle at his spot. When he got there he met Eagle's right hand man Champ and his home girl Lil Shae. It wasn't long before Butch introduced them to Hazel and their crew was formed. From then on there were no fair ones. If you fought one you had to fight them all every time you seen them. The fights escalated to stabbings and the stabbings to gunfights. Once they got to the guns though, they were the bloodiest crew of young ones Roxbury and the South End had ever seen. "Yo Eagle! Eagle!" shouted Butch over the crowd and loud music. "What up nigga!" yelled Eagle, throwing his arms up letting everybody know the young gangsters were there and ready for whatever.

Little did they know they were on a short list of murderous crews being hand picked to control the city and all drug/firearm shipments coming into it. Tree and Cal walked over to the silver Hummer and hopped in the back. "There all here," said the smooth, light skinned cat named Cal. "Butch and his whole crew." "Perfect," said Jahki, with smoke blowing from his nose. "Let them chill for awhile. We'll rap wit them later."

"You got it boss," said Tree, in his deep voice as he and Cal exited the truck.

"Hurt's the god so you gon be the king of this whole shit," said Tyrik while driving down Malcolm X blvd. He was a real militant, husky dude and been chopping up bodies for Jahki going on six years now. "Without loyal soldiers," said Jahki, still smoking his cigarette, "there's no such thing as a king my nigga." "You know I got you till my casket drop homie," said Tyrik. "I know, I know, and its vice versa," said Jahki. "If everybody was as loyal as you man, we'd take over the fucking world," he laughed. Tyrik laughed too as he played a cd on the system. In the back of their minds they knew that what was just said was some true shit, and that's what made it so funny.

One hour later Cal got a call on his cell. "Its show time," he said. "We'll be there in a few minutes." Cal hung the phone up and tapped Tree on his arm, it was time. Tree finished the last of the Bacardi in his plastic cup and they left for Butch and his crew. They were only eight cars up from Tree and Cal and had no idea the two men had been watching them since they arrived. "Yo look who's coming," said Shae. The crew, drinking, smoking and leaning up against the Benz, looked down the street and saw the two men headed their way.

They were from Mattapan and were well known around the city for being ruthless killers in Jahki's army. One of the most respected gangsters in the city, everyone feared his wrath like he was god. When his men approached you it was either to set up a meeting or to kill. The two men hadn't drawn their weapons so the crew knew that a meeting was being called. Something big was going down and they all knew it.

"Ladies and gentlemen," Cal began calmly, "Jahki would like to arrange a meeting with you, tonight." What Cal said wasn't misunderstood. It wasn't a question. It was a statement. "What time and place?" asked Champ, standing firm with his arms crossed. "Now, on Clifton St.," Tree answered. Just then the silver Hummer pulled up beside the Benz. The window on the front passenger went down and there he was smoking a cigarette with a big grin on his face. Jahki. "I've been dieing to meet you," he said, addressing Butch and his crew.

"I love your work. It reminds me of my own when I was a young one. Well don't just stand there being rude, lets go. We have a lot to talk about," he said, with that grin still stretched across his face. "Follow us," said Cal as he hopped in the back of the Hummer. "That's one big mutha fucka," said Eagle, speaking about Tree. "Big giant ass nigga." "That don't mean shit," said Champ. "I got something for niggas like that," he continued, slowly tapping the Desert Eagle he kept on his waist.

"You know what I'm saying?" Lil Shae added on in her deep accent while gripping the tec in her hand bag. Hazel and Butch couldn't help but to laugh as they got in the Benz. "We'll be right behind yall," said Eagle. The three walked quickly to the black Beemer parked a few cars behind the Benz. In no time they were pulling out of their parking spot and driving down the street. The Hummer sped off and so went the Benz followed by the Beemer. Next stop, The Gates of Hell.

CHAPTER 4

Dorchester, Saturday 3/22/09 12:00a

The silver Hummer made a left off Dudley onto Clifton St. Butch and his crew had never been on the street before. They drove by it plenty of times but never down it. Jahki's army packed the street from top to bottom all day everyday ready for war. AK 47's, MAC 10's, MAC 11's, M-16's, AR-15's, sawed off gages and double barrel shotguns were only some of the weapons seen in the hands of the soldiers. The street was a military base.

There were cars parked up and down each side of it to act as shields if it went under attack. Most of the street lights were shot out, all but a few and they were further down toward the center. It was pitch black and all that could be heard were dogs barking. Champ, Lil Shae and Eagle loved every second of it. "They got this shit locked down yo," said Champ from the back seat. "Yeah, this is how you do it," Shae agreed, mesmerized by the whole thing. "If you gon do it, this is how you do it, on some straight military shit."

"Yo, Jahki wanna meet wit us," said Eagle, interrupting the two. "I don't know man but if my thoughts is correct I think he's gon cut us in on some power plays. You know, like hits and shit. Just think about it. He said he like our work. He can't be calling us down here for nothing else." "You right," said Champ, staring at the Benz in front of them. "We do what we do and that's the only reason we here." "Fuck it," said Lil Shae, "If that's what it is then its better for us. I rather be on the nigga side then against him, for real."

Champ and Eagle agreed. They felt where She was coming from. It wasn't fear. It was common sense. The Hummer pulled up to a house that resembled more of a mansion. "This is it," said Hazel, looking Butch in his eyes. Still sipping on his brew he asked, "You strapped?" "You know it," she answered. "Then I guess I'm ready to talk business then," he said. They got out the car and walked up to the tall black gate that surrounded the big house.

Dogs were everywhere, barking and jumping all over the gate. "Don't worry," said Tyrik. "Their trained. Sit down!" he shouted over the loud barking as he opened the gate. At his command the dogs sat still as statues. Jahki walked to the porch slowly and everyone followed. "Wipe your feet before you come in," he said, brushing his shoes on the doormat before entering the house.

CHAPTER 5

Dorchester, Saturday 3/22/09 12:10a

The group walked in silence until they reached two massive doors at the end of the dark hall. Jahki opened the doors, walked up to a large table in the center of the room and took his seat. Butch and his crew entered the room and were shocked at how big and luxurious it was. It was a large dining room. It had hard wood floors, paintings hung from the pitch black walls and a dimly lit chandelier sat right over the table.

Once everyone was seated the meeting began. "I've been expecting you," said Jahki. His grin was now gone and there was only a sheet of ice that covered his black face. Looking across the table at the newcomers, he folded his hands and began slowly. "We want you to work for us. We control all of Dorchester and Mattapan, now we want Roxbury and the South End. You're the heavy hitters down there and that's why you're here."

"We don't want anything to change. We want you to continue doing what you do best and that's keeping order in your sections. You'll have an unlimited supply of a variety of guns, more then enough soldiers and of course more money then you've ever seen in your life coming in weekly. You'll be the generals of the armies in your sections and I'll be the president over you. All orders will come through me and me only unless you get a direct order from Hurt."

"Also, you'll join the ranks of my highest officials. I'm sure you already know who they are but I'll introduce them for those who don't. Tyrik is the general of Dorchester. Tree and Cal are the generals of Mattapan and Hurt is god over us all. He's taking care of some business at the moment and will be here shortly." Jahki was all business. Every word spoken was right to the point.

His generals feared crossing him in any way for fear of what would happen to a once loved and trusted comrade. They would get it worse then anyone else because of how close he let them get. Now Butch and his crew felt exactly what they felt and it chilled them to the bone. This man was not to be crossed.

Butch stared Jahki in his eyes and said, "With an offer like that there's no way we could refuse." He looked at his crew and back at Jahki and said, "We're in." They were now the controllers of the whole city. Just then the big doors opened and in walked Hurt wearing a black suit and trench coat. The man was huge, just about the same size as Tree. He took his seat and in a deep voice asked, "Where are we?" Jahki looked over at him and answered, "We family now." It was now etched in stone, the city was under a new order.

CHAPTER 6

Dorchester, Monday 4/2/09 2:00p

The first half of the plan was complete with control over the last two sections of the city. Next on the list was control over every gun and drug shipment coming in. Now only three people stood in the way of the rising empire. They had two choices, either comply or go to war. A simple game of life or death was being played and Hurt was dealing the cards.

The cell phone on the dresser rang as Jahki stood in the mirror putting his coat on over his grey suit. "Its time," he said to himself as he stared at his face in the mirror. His skin was jet black but his eyes were even darker. His facial expression cold as ice. Standing at six foot two and weighing two hundred and twenty four pounds solid, he resembled a professional boxer. The phone rang one more time before he answered it. "I'm outside," said Hurt before hanging up.

Jahki, still looking at himself in the mirror, fixed his tie, brushed off his coat and left the house. Once the car door closed Hurt leaped from the curb in the black Cadillac. "All those years of ripping and running finally paid off young blood," said Hurt, staring at the big house in the rear view mirror. "I always told you that you were a leader, that you were gonna be the one to bring it all together and now its finally taking place. I waited my whole life to see this shit man. I was born for this," he continued while driving the car through the rainy streets.

"Everything I learned I learned from you man," said Jahki while watching houses pass. "Naw young blood, I might of told you how to do things but you knew how all along. You were a natural. I just had to guide you through a little." "And I appreciate it," said Jahki. Hurt looked at him and said, "Young blood, I was just teaching you how to survive the same way the soldiers taught me when I was your age."

"Now its on you to show these young cats the way. We pass this skill down the same way the Asians pass down martial arts, you know?" Jahki laughed and nodded his head in agreement. The man was a genius. Every time he spoke a jewel was dropped and it was so clear you couldn't misinterpret it. "How you get so wise man?" asked Jahki. "You be sounding like you mad old sometimes, like you a hundred an shit." Hurt turned the radio on and answered him, "I been around for a long time, longer than you think young blood, longer then you think."

Jahki had known the man ever since he was a kid and he still looked the same, he never aged. As far as he could remember Hurt was always around pulling his coat, and he was always right. His instinct was never wrong. It was strange, almost like it was all planned. "Detective Scott understands everything clearly?" asked Jahki, getting back to business.

"Yeah," said Hurt. "We're the only ones he sells guns to in the city and in return he gets a percentage of every gun we sell plus three quarters of a mill up front just for signing the deal." "We've been doing business with him for years, its only right he goes with the program," said Jahki. "Me and Detective Scott go way back and if its one thing I know its that he been dirty, taking blood money since I can remember," said Hurt. "Money is king right?" Jahki asked. Hurt answered, "You ain't never lied young blood. Money is king."

The meeting was suppose to be in the back room of a Chinese restaurant on Dorchester Ave but Detective Scott felt it could've been a set up and wanted to change the meeting place at the last minute. Jahki and Hurt ware already in the back room when they got the call. "OK, so where you wanna meet?" asked Hurt, looking across the little table at Jahki.

"I don't know Hurt, somewhere in the open, you know? This is a big deal I'm signing onto and I want everything to go as planned," said Detective Scott. "Well where are you right now?" asked Hurt. "I'm on Columbia Rd and Washington. I just passed Burger King," said Detective Scott." "Alright then lets say we meet at Franklin Park Zoo," Hurt suggested.

"Perfect, perfect, I'll see you there," agreed Detective Scott. The new meeting spot was great for him. It was in the open. It was daytime and there was a police station not to far from there so if anything went down he could radio for help and try to shoot it out until they arrived. Back at the Chinese food restaurant Jahki and Hurt were waiting for the food they had just ordered. Nothing big, just a trey of fried chicken and spare ribs.

"Fuck it," said Jahki as they sat in the small shadowy room. "If he's gon make us wait then we might as well order something to go. I'm starving anyway." "I dig that," said Hurt. In five minutes they were out of there and headed to the new meeting place. When they arrived Detective Scott was standing beside his car under his umbrella drinking a cup of coffee. "Lets do this," said

Jahki, finishing up the rib he was eating. "Pass me a napkin," said Hurt as he put a chicken bone in the bag the food came in.

When the car doors opened the two men stepped out wiping grease from their hands before opening their umbrellas. "How was lunch?" asked Detective Scott. "Chinese," said Hurt, sarcastically. "Yeah, I know. I asked for that one," said Detective Scott. "Let me introduce you," said Hurt. "Detective Scott this is Jahki. Jahki, Detective Scott." The two men shook hands and the three of them began to walk.

"Do you know the agreement?" asked Jahki. "Do I know it? I memorized it," said Detective Scott. "And you agree with it?" asked Jahki. "Absolutely," answered Detective Scott, before sipping his coffee. "You can't beat the percentages and lets be frank, the three quarters up front is the sealer. We don't make much on the force and never did so I always said fuck it. If I'm gonna be out here risking my life I'm walking away with more then enough to retire with, you know?"

"Smart man," said Jahki as they stopped and stared at the zebras behind the gate. "With the deal we're giving you you'll be set for life and will still be making money long after you retire. We just need you to move the shipments to us and only us. We'll take care of the rest from there." "You know what Jahki?" asked Detective Scott. "I've been watching you since you first started running with Hurt and I can see why he took you under the wing, you two are just alike. Unfucking believable, really. I'm in on the agreement but I have one question. What about the other guys who get shipments from me, what are you gonna do about them?"

"We control them and the few we don't, fuckem. They'll either play by our rules or they won't play at all," said Jahki. "You don't leave much of a choice there do you?" asked Detective Scott. "No," Jahki answered. "I wasn't taught that way." The three men continued to talk business as they finished touring the zoo. When they were done they drove to the exit side by side. Jahki handed Detective Scott a suitcase. They shook hands and the Caddy disappeared in the heavy rain.

Detective Scott opened the suitcase and flipped through the money carefully. It was all there. Now with that added up with what he'd been saving for years he had a little over five million in cash. "All these years, all of these fucking years. It was all worth it," said Detective Scott as he drove out of the parking lot tightly gripping the suitcase handle. "One down and two to go," said Jahki, while lighting up a cigarette. "But I still don't trust that fucken pig." Hurt just laughed. He already knew the detectives future and it wasn't a bright one.

CHAPTER 7

South Boston, Tuesday 4/3/09 5:00a

The cordless phone rang loudly breaking Lt Chang's morning meditation. "What happened now?" he asked as he picked the phone up and read the caller ID. It was Detective Scott, that could only mean one thing. The first deal was made and a new order was officially rising to take control of the city. Lt Chang had been waiting for this for years now and had his own ideas of how he wanted things to play out. "Good morning sir," said Lt Chang, while lifting his mug for a sip of tea.

"Good morning," said Detective Scott. "It's a go. We finally got these slimy fucks where we want them. Once you and Silma close your deals the balls in our court, then we can finally get close enough to kill both Hurt and Jahki and put who we want in their positions." "Yes. I do believe everything is going to go just as smoothly as we planned," said Lt Chang. "I am going to meet with this Jahki later on today and close my deal accordingly. Like clock work he'll die when he meets Dr Silma. If its true what you say and Hurt is with him at the last meeting then they'll finally fall and the city will be ours."

"Trust me Lt, Hurt will be there. Jahki's a mean son of a bitch but Hurts the ringleader," said Detective Scott. "And he will pay dearly for it," said Lt Chang. "I would love to sit and chat but I have to be going now detective." "All right Lt, you take it easy," said Detective Scott. "I'll try," answered the Lt as he hung the phone up. Things were going to go one way or the other. It was all just a matter of time. Lt Chang finished up his tea, grabbed his car keys off the counter and left for work.

He was the Head of Security at Boston Medical Center and had been for twelve years now. He was a very stern man and didn't take shit from nobody. Responsible for the lives of everyone at the hospital, he couldn't take his job lightly. Lt Chang was a leader. His soldiers respected him and would go to war for him at a moments notice. But like every man in the city, he was corrupt. He was the only heroin supplier in the city.

His dope was pure, fresh from Cambodia. He made millions off the stuff but there was only one problem, he didn't want to continue doing business with any and every hustler looking to deal weight. It was a hassle. Plus he didn't want it to be linked back to him in any way. Even though he distributed it through his soldiers it was still too close. Doing business with a single organization would be perfect. That way they would be in charge of portioning the drugs throughout the city.

CHAPTER 8

South End, Tuesday 4/3/09 6:00p

"Thank you for calling Boston Medical Center, this is Eva speaking, how may I help you?" asked the young lady at the service desk. "Yes, I would like to speak to Lt Chang," said Tyrik. "Hold for one minute please" she responded. Tyrik was on hold for about twelve seconds, then a mans voice came through the phone. "This is Lt Chang, how may I help you?" "You could help me a lot Lt," answered Tyrik as he threw large pieces of raw steak at the guard dogs from the front porch of the big house. "My boss would like to speak to you if your not too busy."

"I am actually just getting off right now so tell him that it would be a pleasure to meet with him as soon as possible," said Lt Chang. "That would be great," said Tyrik, still throwing steaks at the hungry dogs. "Hold on one second Lt." Suddenly Jahki was on the phone, "Hello." "Hello," responded the Lt.

"This must be Jahki? I've heard so much about you." "I hope not all bad things," said Jahki. "No, no, there actually good things," said the Lt. "That's good to hear," Jahki laughed. "So Lt, When and where?"

"My home," answered Lt Chang. "We could sit down and have a face to face if that's ok with you?" "That's the best thing I've heard all day," said Jahki. "Where's the location?" "Andrew station in twenty minutes," answered Lt Chang. "Twenty minutes it is," said Jahki as he hung up Tyriks cell. "What's the word?" asked Tyrik, while lighting up a cigarette. "Face to face, Andrew station in twenty," said Jahki. "So you want me to wait outside?" asked Tyrik. "Yeah, me and the dope man gotta seal the deal. You know the routine, anything funny, you grab the ax, chop the house down and everything outside of it," said Jahki.

"My pleasure boss," said Tyrik as he headed to the Hummer. He didn't want anything funny to go down with Jahki but he still wanted to kill up some more shit with that AK he kept on the front seat. Already dressed in a suit, Jahki grabbed his overcoat and made his way to the truck. Destination, Andrew station.

South Boston

Standing outside of the truck the two men smoked cigarettes and watched the scenery. This was the side of town where the policemen, soldiers and Dr's lived. It sure was nice and clean, nothing like the hood. In five minutes Lt Chang was spotted coming from around the corner. "That's him," said Tyrik. "That's him in the uniform." Jahki turned his head and said, "Yeah, there that nigga go." Lt Chang had to be at least six feet, one hundred and eighty pounds.

"What gave me away?" asked Lt Chang, looking around at the busy intersection. "We the only niggas out here," said Jahki as he shook the Lt's hand. "You have a point," laughed Lt Chang. "Who's your friend?" "Tyrik," Jahki answered. "He'll be waiting outside if you don't mind." "Alright then, lets talk business. You can pull right around the corner. My house is the one way in the back," said Lt Chang as he and Jahki began walking to the house.

They say that by looking someone in the eyes you can tell a lot about them. What the Lt seen in Jahki was more then he had perceived. He expected some arrogant, young maniac but he was wrong. Jahki was calm, cool, calculated and respectful. This made all the difference. Now the Lt felt as though his plan would definitely be unstoppable. As the two men walked down the driveway to the house, Lt Chang stopped Jahki and said, "Before we walk in there I just want to let you know that you are being watched by my men also, so be mindful of how you move your arms."

Jahki glanced at the house to his right and seen a window cracked open on the second floor. The shade was down but one blind was slanted just to show him that he was under the scope. Tyrik figured there were two but there were at least four snipers aimed at him alone. It was business, everyone had to watch their back. "With that being said, lets talk business," said Lt Chang. "Lets talk," Jahki agreed. When they entered the house the smell of incense was in the air mixed with the steam from the water that cooked on the stove.

The two men sat down and Jahki began. "We would like to be the only ones you do business with Lt. We'll even pay a little extra to make the deal that much sweeter. We can move it all. We have the man power. We have the control. We have the whole city. There's no competition." "I am aware of that," said Lt Chang. "But you have one competitor that you are not aware of." "Who?" asked Jahki, curious to know who he was speaking of. "Detective Scott," answered the Lt.

"He has been planning to kill both you and Hurt from the beginning so that he can put his own men in your positions and take control of your operation. I have been in agreement with him the whole time as not to arouse any suspicion, but I've had my own set of plans. Quite frankly I suggest that you kill him before the last meeting with Dr Silma where he'll most likely have protection around." "But he's the main gun runner in the city. How would I get his connect?" asked Jahki.

"I am what you would call, his connect. All of the major weaponry that he sells comes from me first and always has," said Lt Chang. "That fucken worm. If I knew that I would've been killed him," said Jahki as he leaned back in the leather sofa. "No. You couldn't have because at the time I needed him," said the Lt. "But now with your organization taking control of the trades he is of no use to me and a traitor to you."

"Enough said, he's history," said Jahki. "Are there anymore secrets I should know about?" "No. That's all. The waters done, would you like some tea?" asked Lt Chang as he headed to the kitchen. "Yes, I would, thank you," said Jahki, breathing in the sweet smelling incense while letting what he just heard sink in. "Would you like sugar in your tea or no?" asked the Lt. "Three scoops please," said Jahki, glancing around the room for the fourth time. He felt comfortable around the Lt but he never let his guard down for anyone, not even his soldiers.

It was still day light outside. Jahki stood up and looked out the window at Tyrik. Hands down he was one of Jahki's most loyal soldiers. He looked back at Jahki and nodded his head. Jahki nodded back, the deal was done. "Your tea," said Lt Chang, handing Jahki the small cup. His accent was strong but his English was very clear. Jahki couldn't believe it. As he sipped his tea he thought, *this man was the gun connect the whole time.*

It was genius. It was a move that he himself would've made. The only thing on his mind now was Detective Scott. The detective didn't know it yet but he was about to be hunted by every general in Jahki's army. Tree, Ali and Tyrik had already killed for him. Now it was Butch and his crews turn. They were young but also the most vicious and this was the moment they'd been waiting for. It was good as done, Detective Scott was a dead man.

CHAPTER 9

South Boston, Tuesday 4/3/09 7:15p

Jahki finished his tea and placed the cup in the kitchen sink. "Thank you," he said, while turning from the sink, "thank you for everything." "Your welcome," said Lt Chang, still staring out the window. "I'll see you tomorrow," said Jahki as he walked over and gave the Lt a strong handshake. "I will definitely be seeing you tomorrow." "Yes," said Lt Chang, "and hopefully that will be the last we both see of our friend."

Once in the truck Jahki briefed his comrade on everything and ordered a meeting with his generals for yesterday. Tyrik wasted no time contacting them. The boss was first, already at the big house with a crew counting bags of blood money, he was in place. Next was Cal. Tree would be with him nine times out of ten and if he wasn't Cal would lose no time finding him.

Mattapan

The body fell in the trunk of the Cadillac with a loud thud when a phone began to ring. "Is that his phone or yours?" asked Tree, before he burst out laughing. "I think its his man," said Cal, wearing a sinister grin. Pulling the cell phone out of his pants pocket he answered quickly, "Hotep." "Hotep Family, the big house, you and Tree, asap," said Tyrik in a calm tone. "You got it chief," said Cal. "What was that about?" asked Tree as he opened the driver door. "I'm not sure but by judging the way Tyrik just sounded there might be another mutha fucka in this trunk before ten o'clock," said Cal as he jumped in the front passenger seat.

"Fuck it Sundance, lets build a pyramid out these mutha fuckas," said Tree, while starting the car. "This is a nice Caddy," said Cal, lightly rubbing the leather armrest. "This is real nice. Black paint, black leather, wood grain, chrome rims an the whole nine. Hurt need to let me hold onto this bitch man. I'd take real good care of her." "I know you would homie but it a never happen. This his pride and joy. Man probably done had more bodies in it then the coroners," said Tree as he put the car in gear and slowly crept out the garbage filled vacant lot.

Roxbury

When Butch's cell phone rang he was at home having dinner with his mother. "Please make it quick," said Niah, while staring at her son through her glasses. "What's poppen?" asked Butch with his mouth full of spaghetti. "Round up your crew and meet me at the big house," said Tyrik, just arriving at the house himself. "Roger that," said Butch as he hung up the phone. Tyrik laughed to himself, "This mutha fucka picks the wrong times to crack jokes." But you had to love it, that was Butch.

After finishing the rest of his food he kissed his mother on the forehead and was out the door. Inside the Benz he called Hazel's cell. When she picked up he heard R&B in the background and knew she was still busy. "What up cuz?" asked Hazel while smoking a blunt. "There's some shit going down and we being called to the big house so be outside when I get there," he said.

The South End

Hanging up the phone she put both of her hands behind the head of the man who was eating her out. She was just about to climax, just a few more seconds. Wrapping her thick thighs around his neck she bussed all over his face while grinding her wet pussy on his mouth. The more she moaned the more he ate her out. "OK I gotta go baby," cried Hazel as she climbed out the bed and grabbed her clothes.

"Go ahead shorty, do you, I got mines for the night," said the young man. He was right. He'd bust three times already, got his dick sucked and ate some good pussy for about an hour. As far as he was concerned he was straight. Hazel felt the same. She bussed double what he did in her first couple of hours with him.

While she got dressed he couldn't help but to stare. She was bad, thick in all the right places and pretty as shit. "Yo Hazel, holla at me when you freed up," said the young man as he lit up the blunt she had just put in the ashtray. "Alright," laughed Hazel while hurrying out the front door. She couldn't front, she was catching feelings for the boy. He was cool but she never told him anything or let him get in the way of her business. She kept it hood. Business always came first before play.

Downstairs Butch had just pulled up. "Whats going on?" asked Hazel as she jumped in the car. "I don't know. I got the call to round up the troops. I just got off the phone wit Shae. She wit Eagle at the range and said Champ's somewhere in Uphams Corner taking care of some things. They should be at the big house before us cause they only a few blocks away from there," explained Butch. None of them knew what was going on but they knew it involved them, and whatever involved them always involved homicide.

CHAPTER 10

Dorchester, Tuesday 4/3/09 7:40p

Everyone sat quietly at the table in the dimly lit room waiting for the bosses to start the meeting. "Shit done hit the fan," said Tyrik. "The mutha fucken gun connect been plotten to x out the bosses an take over the organization," he continued. "Shits goin down tonight. Jahki said he want that nigga in pieces, you heard?" They all nodded their heads in agreement as they listened closely. After Tyrik gave them the run down the room fell silent and nothing was said for a while. The shit had definitely hit the fan.

A few minutes passed before the bosses entered through the big doors. The room was cold before they got there but now it seemed to be as cold as it could ever get. Eagle didn't know who the gun connect was and didn't give a fuck. Either way he was assed out because nobody crossed Hurt. If Hurt was god,

Jahki was Jesus Christ and in this version he and his disciples were holding the nails and hammers.

The two men took their seats and Jahki got straight to business. "Ladies and gentlemen, you were called here tonight because we have a problem. An old business partner's been plotten to wipe out our operation. I'm sure you all know the history, Hurt built this organization. We all sit at this table because of him. Without him there would be no fucken table. There would be no power. There would be no money. There would be no unity and there would be no order."

"I want this faggot dead tonight. If you could bring him in alive that would be cool but if you can't then bring him in pieces, you hear me? Bring me his head. Don't take no small joints either. Tyrik, only choppers. You, Tree and Cal, close him in. Butch, if yall can bring him here, bring him here. If you can't, do him and anyone wit him. I don't give a fuck if he got nuns wit him, you hear me? Bringem in bags. Whatever stash you find on him or at his spot is yours. Yall split that. We got a big meeting to attend tomorrow morning so yall got all night." Looking at his watch he said, "Its eight o'clock family, lets get to work."

The meeting was adjured. Orders were given and were to be executed. Everyone exited the room but Jahki and Hurt. They remained seated and spoke privately in the dark room. About what? No one knew and didn't wish to. That was their business and in their line of work minding your business was a cardinal rule everyone followed religiously, especially the generals.

Outside the doors Tyrik took the crew down the wide hall to what looked like a walk in closet. Once inside the small room he hit a light switch that revealed a set of stairs leading to the basement. Tree and Cal were already aware of them. They'd been down them many of times and knew exactly what waited at the bottom. Butch and his crew didn't know what was down there but from what they just heard Jahki tell Tyrik, they figured he was taking them to the guns and they were right.

As soon as they hit the basement floor they seen an arsenal of guns hanging from the walls. The floor was tiled with white marble. The walls and ceiling were both ultra white so that every gun hanging was completely visible. There were boxes of ammunition placed underneath every separate gun section. In the middle of the room sat six long black tables covered with RPG's followed by six more of the same tables covered with grenades and bullet proof vests.

Champ estimated that there had to be over one thousand guns in the room alone and at least one hundred thousand rounds of ammunition, and knowing how Hurt and Jahki got down, this was only one of numerous gun spots they had placed all over the city. No doubt about it, they had money and business sense to go with it. "All right niggas, yall heard the man, choppers only!" yelled Tyrik, pointing at the wall with the AK's on it. Everyone grabbed one and a few clips. They all had the same idea, dead or alive he was coming home tonight.

"Yo where the saws at?" asked Lil Shae, while looking around the room. Tree stared at her in awe. *How could this petite little chick be so ruthless*, he thought. Tyrik and Cal shook their heads probably thinking the same as Tree. Cal couldn't hold it in. He looked at Shae and said, "Yo, you really cooked." "Ha. Naw nigga, you ain't seen cooked," she said, staring Cal dead in his eyes. "Watch what I do to your boy when I catch him." "Yeah right, that ain't my boy," he laughed.

Everyone followed in joking and talking shit about the target. Out of all nights, this was absolutely the worst night to be him or anyone even next to him. "Everybody straight?" asked Tyrik. They all nodded yes while strapping on bullet proofs. "The target is Detective Scott. He lives off of Dorchester Ave all the way down before you get to South Boston. I been there wit

Hurt a couple of times to pick up some of the guns you see in this room. He's a fat fuck. Looks just like Santa Clause."

" You can't miss him, he got grey hair and a big grey beard. Yall niggas already know who he is. You just didn't know he was the gun connect. I'm sure you also know not to sleep on him cause he a one shot kill wit that forty cal. But fuck all that. He got one hammer to our eight. Ain't no way he surviving the hit. Jahki got all the blocks looking out for him already. Nobody ain't seen him yet so he want us to check his apartment first."

"When we do find out where he's at, me, Tree and Cal is gon play the background and keep yall covered. If yall can bring him in alive then bring him in but if you can't then murk him where you catch him. The spot he die in is the spot we choppen him in. Since you called it first, Shae, you got his head. The saws is in the corner over there in that green army bag on top of the butcher block. Everyone grab one and lets be out. Oh yeah, we all in the Hummer so yall be easy wit them shits man. I just got that bitch washed and vacuumed this morning and I don't want no cuts on the seats."

"Shotgun!" yelled Butch as he grabbed a saw out of the bag. "I got a wing yo, I got a wing." "Yeah me too," said Champ. "Fuck it I'll take a leg," said Eagle. "I'll do a leg too," said Hazel. "I guess that leaves us three to break up the torso," said Tree. "It don't make me no never mind," said Cal. "I'll do the belly, you and Tyrik do the rib cage." It was all a contest to them, who could be the most savage.

Statistically, Hurt was. He'd been killing far longer than any of them could ever imagine. He was the best at what he did. Jahki came next because he trained under him. The rest of them fell right under Jahki. All of them extremely dangerous. Each one a monster in their own way. Each one hand picked by the man himself. With them working in unison under his guidance they were unstoppable and therefore it was only right they control the natural order of their world.

CHAPTER 11

Dorchester, Tuesday 4/3/09 8:15p

Now piled in the truck the hunt was on. First stop, Detectives Scotts house. As the truck jumped from the curb the crew looked through the tinted windows. Groups of soldiers guarding the house stared back. Raising their guns in the air they saluted the generals. The word was out. They were being sent to hit the the precincts MVP. Death was inevitable.

It only took ten minutes to arrive around the corner from the detectives house. Night had fallen and they were at the advantage. If the detective was home there'd be no way he could escape the ambush. Lil Shae and Hazel were up. Being females they wouldn't arouse much suspicion walking down the street at this time of night. They would easily be mistaken for prostitutes.

As they got around the corner they noticed that the street itself was quiet but the bar on the corner was loud. Music blasted from inside and people were heard laughing and conversing. As they continued down the street they noticed the back door to the bar was open and that was why they heard everything so clearly. They began looking around to see if they could spot the dark blue Crown Vic. Halfway down the street Hazel remembered that there was a car with a cover over it behind the bar.

"Shae," she whispered, "go check if the car behind the bar is it and I'm gon check behind the house to see if its back there." "Alright," said Shae. She could feel it, they were close. A group of females came strolling out the back of the bar for some fresh air. Shae knew they would be a while so she sat on one of the porches two houses down across the street from where they were. There was a van blocking her from the groups view so they never knew she was there.

Meanwhile, down the street Hazel just got in front of Detective Scotts house. He lived in a three family building on the second floor. She snuck around the house to see if any lights were on in his apartment but she saw nothing. His back yard was connected with his neighbors. There were five cars lined up in an old garage with no doors. She checked every car until she got to the last one.

A smile was creeping on her face when she was startled by a voice. "Yo," Shae whispered, "I checked it. That's not it." She took her eyes off Hazel and looked at the car behind her. That was it, the dark blue Crown Vic. "This niggas over here somewhere," said Hazel, looking at the back of the two houses. "You think he's in the house?" asked Lil Shae. "Naw. All the lights is out up there and it ain't even nine. He's either gone or he's at the bar or something," said Hazel.

"Alright, lets go get the boys and check the house," said Shae. "If he ain't in there we going to the bar." "OK, lets do this shit," said Hazel. When they got back to the truck they didn't have to say a word, the smiles on their faces said it all. "So where he at?" asked Eagle. "We not sure," Shae answered. "He's either sleep in the house, out somewhere or getting fucked up at the bar. Haze found his wheels in back of the house so he might be around here." "Lets make moves then," said Tyrik.

Once the girls got in he drove around the corner and parked in the back, blocking off the Crown Vic. On cue they grabbed their guns and fell out the truck like SWAT. Butch, Lil Shae and Eagle went up the back. Champ, Tyrik and Hazel went up the front and Tree and Cal posted on each side of the house in case the detective tried to escape through a window. Butch counted to three and kicked the back door to the apartment wide open. When Tyrik heard the noise he busted in through the front knocking the door off its hinges.

They swarmed in searching every room for the man but he wasn't there. "He gotta be in the bar man," sad Butch. "This building is fucken empty. I'm telling you, this niggas at the bar yo." "Word," said Champ. "His cars still here. There's a good chance we might catch him at the bar." "Then lets be out," said Eagle. They all ran down the back stairway and went to the truck. "Hazel," said Tyrik, "you and Shae go check out the bar. See what you can see. We'll be right here waiting." "No doubt," said Lil Shae. She was in the zone. If he was in the bar she had something planned for him.

When they got to the bar more people were out back just hanging and enjoying themselves. Hazel walked up and asked the first person she seen smoking for a cigarette. Before she could finish her sentence some guy handed her one he had just lit and got back to his conversation. He didn't give a fuck. It was a party. He was having a good time and had half a pack left anyway. "Thank you," said Hazel as they made their way to the back door.

The place was packed. Shae slid in and began to walk around. Hazel watched her back the whole time. "Go get him Shae," she whispered to herself while smoking her cigarette. "Get that mutha fucka." Shae walked around the whole bar and didn't see nothing. Then, in the back, way in the left corner she saw the man sitting at a table laughing and drinking with a few friends. It was Detective Scott.

She knew his face from seeing him around the way on many occasions. He was always driving by like he was untouchable. All that shit was about to be over now. She left quickly and told Hazel her plan. It was simple. He was in a corner so four would get him and his table while the other four dropped everything that looked like a threat. There were a lot of cops in there. They were in plain clothes all the time now but you could still tell them from other people.

It was all in how they carried themselves. Most were always extra tuff all the time and acted like they were above everything. So instead of risking anybody from the team they would just do the whole bar. "I love how you think," laughed Hazel. "You just so fucken evil." "And sexy too," said Lil Shae. "Oh yeah," said Hazel, "you a bad bitch." "No," laughed Lil Shae, "*we,* some bad bitches baby. *We.*" Strutting and joking around they celebrated all the way back to the truck.

As soon as Tree seen them he asked, "What's good?" "He in there," Shae answered as she and Hazel put on their bullet proofs. "He in the far left corner at a table with three little pigs. There's mad pork in there yo. No bullshit, real deep, laughing it up too." "Not for long," said Eagle. He was tired of waiting. He'd been vexed since they first got the call at the range. Shae was killing him in the shooting contest they were having and talking cash shit when the call came in. If he could, he was going to try to keep the fat man alive just so he could be tortured.

"Yo lets do this. I'm tired of waiten man," said Champ. "Yeah the suspense is killen me," said Tree. He looked pissed off and blunted but still a hundred percent. "Lets go," said Cal. "Shae. You, me, Champ and Eagle get the big man and yall work on the bar," said Hazel. "Yeah, that sounds like a perfect plan. Lets get it," said Tree as he started walking from behind the house. Everyone followed in formation, they were organized.

Same as last time, just more crucial. Four went in the front and four went in the back. The people hanging outside the bar lucked up that night. They took off running and didn't look back. Eagle waited for a second outside the open front entrance and peeked in. He looked around real quick to see exactly where the man was sitting because if he made one mistake the one shot kill would be the last thing he saw.

Like a professional hit man he quickly stepped through the door pointing the gun directly in Detective Scotts face before blowing his partners forehead off, throwing blood, brains and skull fragments flying through the air. People in between Eagle and Detective Scott hit the floor screaming. Lil Shae, Champ and Hazel moved in swiftly killing the other two at the table before they could even think about grabbing their guns. Everyone in the bar was yelling at the top of their lungs and running for the doors. The four shooters swarmed in on the detectives table, now killing everyone around it. Frozen with fear and intoxicated, Detective Scott went for his gun and fired a head shot at Eagle missing him by an inch.

Lil Shae shot him in his legs through the top of the table. When he fell to the floor Champ kicked the table over on him. He fired three loud shots through the table hitting Champ in the stomach causing him to stumble to the floor in pain. Outraged, Hazel fired at his kneecaps almost taking the shins off completely. The man let out a sharp cry while grabbing at his bleeding legs. Eagle saw the detectives gun slide from under the table aiming to take another shot at them and fired at Scotts wrist knocking the gun loose. "He almost caught me," said Eagle, looking Shae in the face. While helping Champ remove his vest and get on his feet, she looked back still shocked "Yeah, almost."

Any other day Detective Scott would've retrieved his weapon a lot faster but today wasn't that day. Eagle was too fast and the detective was scared shitless and drunk. The deadly combination proved to be fatal. He'd never seen anyone move a big gun so fast in his life and he never expected out of all places to be ambushed around the corner from his home. Yet and still he managed to let off four accurate shots. Eagle dodged a bullet, but Champ wasn't so lucky. Had it not been for that vest he might not have survived.

All the while they were trapping the detective the other four were shooting anyone who looked like a cop. Shae kept the gun on the crippled detective while her three comrades took part in the blood bath. Some people ran for the restroom but Butch seen them and went to run in after them. Shots flew from the bathroom tearing up the whole door. Butch fell to the floor and rolled out of the way of the gun fire. Armed officers fled to the restroom, regrouped and created a stronghold in the midst of all the confusion.

The young shooters traded rounds with the officers for what seemed like forever until no more shots came from the restroom. After a moment of silence stilled the air Butch pushed open the door and to his surprise there were a few people still alive in the room. The terrified officers holding empty guns begged for their lives but their words fell on deaf ears. "Naw. Orders is orders," he laughed before opening fire on the men pressed against the urinals. Cold blooded. Every officer in the bar was considered with the detective and by law they were united as one and orders *were* orders. "*Do him and anyone wit him.*"

CHAPTER 12

Dorchester, Tuesday 4/3/09 9:30p

Detective Scott screamed as Tree dragged him by his arm out of the bar. The three men who sat with him were taken as well. They were all cops, fully equipped with automatic hand guns and badges. Tyrik pulled up to the back of the bar and yelled out, "The bags is in the back seat!" "This nigga got body bags?" asked Champ. Cal opened the back passenger door, picked them up and let them fall to the floor. "Yeah," he answered, "heavy duty ones too. You could fit two people in them."

Everybody helped stuff a body in a bag and throw it in the truck. Even though he was alive, after kicking him in his face a few times, Tyrik zipped the detective up in a bag too. He wasn't going to die yet. Tyrik just figured he'd fuck wit him until he got him to the house. "Yall go check his spot and one of us is gon come back to scoop you," said Cal as he jumped in the truck wit Tyrik and Tree.

Butch and his crew walked down the street, choppers still in their hands, back to Detective Scotts apartment. When they got there they searched the apartment from head to toe, emptying out dressers, cabinets and closets. Cutting open mattresses, box springs and sofas while busting open TV's and radios. They found nothing. "What the fuck!" yelled Eagle. "This nigga got it hid somewhere else!" "Naw, be cool. There's something. Its either in here or his wip," said Hazel, trying to calm him down and herself at the same time.

Lil Shae started ripping apart his fridge and Champ went in the pantry to check the deep freezer. Preoccupied with all the other rooms in the apartment no one had searched the pantry, not even once since they searched the apartment the first time looking for the detective. The freezer had a pad lock on it so he stepped back and took a shot at it knocking it right off. Everyone ran over to see what he was shooting at and there it was, inside the deep freezer, cold hard cash, big bags of it. They pulled them out and brought them in the living room. "We got some bread now," said Butch.

"That's what's up," said Jahki, from the hallway surprising everyone in the living room. "It look like all of yall could get right off that. You did good tonight, you did real good. Come on, lets go. Hurt's waiten for you down stairs." They had no idea but Hurt and Jahki were posted across the street from the bar a few minutes after they ran up in the detectives apartment the first time.

Hurt had the whole thing planned. He knew the detectives next move all along so he had him watched almost everywhere he went months before the first meeting. He knew exactly where he was since he got up that morning. He knew where he was all day and where he was going to be later on that night. All it took was a little money and his whereabouts were known on a daily basis. Hurt had half the city on the payroll, even Detective Scott, so he should've known better.

The same man who gave Hazel the cigarette behind the bar was the same man who called Hurt and told him where the detective was at eight o'clock. He worked in the hospital and was the detectives next door neighbor but for two hundred grand he was his shadow when the detective was home. The man knew exactly what was going to happen before he seen Hazel. He already knew hers and Lil Shae's description and was looking out for them. When he seen Hazel he was just going to leave but she ended up asking him for a cigarette anyway. She didn't notice it but right after he gave her the cigarette he and his friends left.

When they got outside they were shocked. Soldiers were dragging bodies out in bags left and right. "What you gon do wit those?" asked Lil Shae. "Those is dog food," said Jahki. "They love it. Its their favorite meal." Sitting in the shinny black Caddy, Hurt motioned for them to come over. They walked over and stood quietly, waiting for him to speak. "How's the reward money?" he asked. "Its all good," said Champ.

"Yeah young blood, it's a nice little bonus. There's gotta be over five mill in them bags there, probably more. Count it at the Big House, find out for yourselves. That ain't nothing though. We got a lot more money to make. I'm impressed, Jahki too. We proud of yall. You did good. I like how you and the boys handled that situation. Yall work good together, actually, better then we thought you would. That's all I gotta say though. I just wanted to give you your props. What? Yall niggas can stop standin there like I'm bout to get out this car and give out hugs cause the shit ain't happenin. Get on out of here. There's two cars waiten for you aroud the corner." "You got it boss," laughed Butch. Hurt just smiled. He now had the city in the palm of his hands and there was no one who could oppose his organization. Order was absolute.

CHAPTER 13

Dorchester, Wednesday 4/4/09 10:00a

Lt Chang and Dr Silma had just arrived at the Big House. Hurt set up the spot for the last meeting and had them escorted there. Jahki had never met Dr Silma. She was a brown skinned Cape Verde women with long, curly black hair. A soldier opened the gate for the two and they made their way to the porch as Jahki came down to greet them. Up close he saw that she looked like a professional model. She was in her mid twenties, had long legs, a pretty face and a silk dress a few shades darker then her skin complexion with the same color high heals and purse.

"How are you Jahki?" asked Lt Chang. "I'm good Lt, and you?" "I feel great," said Lt Chang. After introducing Dr Silma and Jahki they all walked to the porch. "Is Detective Scott going to be here?" asked Lt Chang, sarcastically. He and the Dr had already heard the news last night. Everyone knew what happened, it was all over the tv. "DIRTY COPS AND INNOCENT CIVILIANS SLAIN IN DORCHESTER BAR. DRUG TRANSACTION GONE BAD. BPD NOW UNDER INVESTIGATION!" "Yes. He's actually in the back playing with the dogs. He loves animals," said Jahki.

Detective Scott was in pieces all over the back yard. Last night Hurt took his time torturing what little life the man had left. When he was done he and Jahki sawed him to pieces and threw him to the dogs. They'd been feeding them all night. There was no meat left on the bones but the dogs were still biting on them. "Lt Chang, Dr Silma, today you'll be meeting my boss and captains. They've all been waiting patiently to meet you," said Jahki.

"Ah, so the plot thickens. That's great," said Lt Chang, "because Dr Silma was just informing me of someone who would very much like to meet with you and your organization." "Really, and just who exactly might that be Dr Silma?" asked Jahki. "He's a businessman a lot like your self Jahki," said Dr Silma. "He's from Cape Verde, my country. He's an honest and fair man. He has much to offer. You'd like him." "I probably would," said Jahki. "You know what? If meeting him meant that I would first have to have dinner with you then yes I probably would like to meet him. What do you think Dr Silma?"

She smiled and turned to Lt Chang. "Lt, you didn't tell me your friend was so charming." Looking back at Jahki she answered his question. "If I have to make you go to dinner with me just to get you to meet with my boss then I guess I really have no say in the matter do I Jahki?" "No. I'm sorry Dr Silma, you don't" he replied, staring deep into her eyes. "Now, ladies and gentlemen, lets start this meeting. I'm sure we all have a lot to talk about."

LaVergne, TN USA
25 February 2011
218047LV00001B/5/P

9 781608 449347